Happy
Birthday,
Lulu!

To Albert
with love

You can also read
Hello, Lulu
ISBN 0-8027-8712-6

and
Lulu's Busy Day
ISBN 0-8027-8716-9

Copyright © 2000 by Caroline Uff

First published in the United States of America in 2000 by Walker Publishing Company, Inc.
First published in Great Britain in 2000 by Orchard Books, London

Library of Congress Cataloging-in-Publication Data available upon request.

PRINTED IN SINGAPORE
2 4 6 8 10 9 7 5 3 1

Happy Birthday, Lulu!

Caroline Uff

Walker & Company
New York

This is Lulu.

Is it your birthday today, Lulu?

"Hello, Lulu,"
says the mail carrier.
"I have so many cards
for you!"

At breakfast
Lulu gets a
birthday
hug

and
a big present.

What's inside?

"Come and play with my new Noah's Ark," says Lulu.

The animals go in two by two.

Brring, brring!
Grandpa calls to wish
Lulu a very special day.

Lulu is busy cooking for her party. Mmm, that smells good.

Teddy has fun blowing
up balloons.
Puff, puff,
puff.

Lulu helps set the table.

It's time for Lulu to get dressed for her party.

Even Teddy has a
red ribbon to wear.
You look
beautiful,
Lulu.

Here come Lulu's friends.

"Thank you!" says Lulu as everyone gives her presents.

Dum dee dum,
dee dum,
dee
dum!

Lulu loves
musical chairs.

Yum yum, it's time for cake. Everyone sings,

"Happy Birthday, dear Lulu.
Happy Birthday to you!"